TEMPTATIONS

VOLUME 1

A collection of erotic stories

Edited by Miranda Forbes

Published by Accent Press Ltd – 2009
ISBN 9781907016288

Printed and bound in the UK

Cover design by
Red Dot Design

Contents

Bliss
by Elizabeth Cage

I had mixed feelings about selling my lovely garden flat in a quiet country cul-de-sac, but I'd just been offered a job in London, a real career move, lots of dosh. I didn't fancy commuting – been there, done that when I was ten years younger – so it made sense to find a place in town. I didn't expect it would be hard to sell, and the estate agent said they had a lot of interest in my property.

Rhiddian Davies was the first person to view. We'd arranged a Sunday morning, not too early (I like my beauty sleep), 11.30 a.m. to be precise. The other prospective buyers were scheduled to view after lunch. At 11.29 a.m., the doorbell rang. I like punctuality.

'Katy Bliss?' He was trying not to smile at the name. I was used to it. Besides, I adored that Welsh accent, the wonderful musical lilt, the delicious way he pronounced the words. I was a sucker for accents, had a thing about them.

'Rhiddian? Come in,' I replied. I gestured him through the door, noticing his long, slim legs in tight jeans, and close-cropped dark hair. He stretched out his hand for me to shake, and I noticed how long and elegant the fingers were. I wondered what his job was. Certainly not a manual one.

'Mind if I take my jacket off? It's raining hard out there.' He slipped the leather biker jacket over his shoulders to reveal a black racer back vest – and a series of tattoos across both shoulders and down his back, a mixture of Japanese Kanji, exotic symbols and a colourful picture of entwined lovers.

'Wow. They look impressive,' I murmured, wanting instinctively to run my fingers over them, tracing the beautiful shapes.

'You like tattoos?'

I nodded. I loved tattoos on men. More than loved. I had a real fetish about them. The more the better. 'What do they mean?'

He touched his right shoulder. 'This means Music. This one is Serenity.'

I hoped he would peel off his vest so I could see all the tattoos that ran down his back. Behave yourself, Katy, I told myself. This guy is a total stranger. He'll think you're a nutcase. But the combination of his gorgeous sexy accent and these tattoos – it was like all my Christmases had come at once. Come being the operative word. Trying to maintain an air of professional composure, I said briskly, 'Well, you'll be wanting to view the flat. Follow me. As you can see this is the kitchen. Small but functional.'

The walls were painted a clinical white and it was furnished with chrome units. Very functional, not feminine, my friends had told me on numerous occasions. I pointed out the fitted fixtures, my mind elsewhere. 'Washing machine and fridge. Cooker. All staying. The place I'm buying is brand new, has all these things.' The window was wide open but my kitchen felt rather hot all of a sudden. 'Would you like a drink?' I asked, feeling very thirsty.

'Mmm, yes please. Something cold.'

I opened the fridge, the waft of chilled air invigorating and welcome. 'Coke?'

'Great.'

'I'll put plenty of ice in it.'

He took it gratefully and sipped. Whereas I, intoxicated by his voice, gulped mine back, the dark frothy liquid dribbling down my mouth, tracing a journey down my chin and neck, and into the deep crevice between my breasts. I wondered if he noticed, part of me hoping he had. But he was probably too polite and ignored the rapidly

3

forming coke stain on my white T-shirt.

'The neighbours are friendly,' I said casually. 'I've been here several years and I shall miss the place, but needs must. What about you?'

'I've been travelling in Europe the past year, so when I got back I rented, until I decided if I wanted to stay here or not. Think I will, if I find the right place to buy. But if I change my mind, I could always rent the place out.' He'd finished his drink already and I downed another, aware that I was still thirsty.

'Want to see the rest of the place? The bathroom's there. Again, compact but well designed. Power shower, sink, loo. Bath of course.'

'I like that it's all white. Clean and bright.'

He was standing close enough to touch, the smell of his sweat mixed with a citrus scent, a heady mixture.

'And this is the bedroom.' My tongue lingered on the word and I hoped he didn't notice.

'That's big,' he commented, his eyes falling on my huge queen-size bed.

'I like big things,' I replied, blushing at how crass that sounded.

'Really?' he grinned.

'And this is the lounge,' I continued, moving on hastily. 'I think it's a good size too.'

Still grinning, he scanned the room, approving of the plasma-screen TV, expensive hi-fi system, dark blue leather sofa and matching blinds and polished wooden floor.

'Very nice.' He paused, considering his next sentence. 'But I didn't expect to see one of those in here.'

'I wondered when you'd say something. You can hardly miss it, I suppose. And no, it's not here to hold up the ceiling, in case you were wondering. No structural problems here.'

'Clearly.' And he glanced at my breasts.

'Don't worry, I'll take it down before I leave. If there are any marks on the ceiling they'll be made good.'

'Are you a pole dancer then?'

'No. I do it for exercise. It's great for fitness, very popular exercise for women. Builds up upper-body strength and thigh grip.' What was wrong with me today? He must think I was a raging nympho.

'I can imagine,' he replied. 'I bet you look amazing on that pole. I'd love to see you dance,' he added. Of course, I had heard that corny line many times before, when I had brought men back home with me – which of course makes me sound even more of a sex addict. But when he said it … was it really so difficult to refuse that hypnotic

5

voice?

'Sit down then,' I replied, my voice taking command. 'I'll give you a dance.'

At first he stared at me open-mouthed, not sure how to respond to this. Was I joking? Winding him up? I put some music on and messed about round the pole, feeling unexpectedly self-conscious. I was wearing a short denim skirt, my feet bare, toes painted slut-red. Slowly, his eyes still registering disbelief, he sat down on the leather sofa and watched as I started to move sinuously around the pole, pivoting, circling, spinning, caressing the pole with my legs, my hands, rubbing my body against it, dancing for him. He soon appeared to be captivated as I climbed and inverted, the moves flowing seamlessly into each other. I had been learning to pole dance for four years, and I loved it. I ran my fingers through my long black hair, down my face and my body, pushing my firm breasts together, my hips snaking. Seeing the lust in his eyes gave me a massive buzz. I had forgotten that this was a stranger who was thinking of buying my flat. My head was somewhere else. Very, very slowly and gradually, I peeled off my T-shirt, high on adrenalin. To my delight, he was transfixed. Then I began to slip down the silky straps of my red and white polka-dot bra, though still keeping my breasts covered, teasing. He reached out a hand. I shook my head sternly.

'No touching.'

Like a naughty schoolboy who has been told off by the teacher, he sank back on the sofa, hands obediently by his sides. I climbed up my pole, crossed my ankles and, finally, pushed my bra down to my waist, revealing my brown nipples, which were already hard. All the time, I retained eye contact with him, noting his expressions, his reactions to the impromptu display he was getting. I slid down the pole and continued the dance, unhooking my bra. But instead of tossing it to the floor, I stepped towards him and, in a quick movement, wrapped it around his wrists, tying them securely.

He gasped, 'What are you doing?'

'What does it look like? I'm seducing you.'

'You're doing a great job,' he muttered under his breath. I could feel his heart beating faster, his breathing more rapid now. I pushed his legs wide apart and occupied the space I had created, swivelling my hips, grinding my thighs, touching my breasts. I was loving every minute and I could see he was too. I leaned forwards, brushed my lips down the flies of his now-tighter trousers. I unzipped him, my fingers circling, squeezing. I felt him grow and swell in my hand and it gave me a feeling of power, which turned me on more. Big time. I had control over his cock – and his pleasure. And the more powerful I felt, the more aroused I got, and the more aroused I got, the bigger he became.

He groaned and as I straddled him, his hungry mouth found my erect nipples, licking and teasing and sucking while my right hand continued to pleasure him. My left hand travelled down his back, clawing at his black, sweat-drenched vest, savouring those amazing tattoos.

Then, without warning, he pulled his hands free and flipped me on to my back. 'Your turn, dirty bitch.' I think the sound of that voice alone could have made me come. His hands, meanwhile, were under my skirt, his long fingers searching for my deep, wet cunt.

'No knickers,' he remarked. 'Slut.' He quickly pushed my legs apart and knelt down between them, tonguing and tasting me, growling and groaning, while tantalising my clit with his thumb and forefinger. I swore and bit, the sensations too intense and raw. I knew I would soon explode, and when I did it would be very, very noisy. Then I came big time, yelling and shouting.

He smiled. 'Hey, maybe that's the real reason you're moving away, your neighbours complained to the council about the noise.'

'Cheeky bastard,' I replied, panting, trying to get my breath back. But before I had a chance, his hand was on the back of my neck, his fingers buried in my long black hair.

'On your knees, cunt,' he growled, tugging on my unruly tresses, forcing me to kneel. He pulled hard, yanking my head back so far that my neck hurt. It sent tremors through my body which culminated in my clit. I adored my hair being pulled – the harder the better – but the only time I had asked a past lover to do this to me, his response had been to tell me how weird I was, so I never asked again. Now, though, allowing this tattooed stranger to behave so brutally towards me, long-buried sensations were triggered and reawakened. He stood in front of me, grinning, increasing the pressure, using his free hand to trace the outline of my lips with surprising gentleness. I wanted to bite his fingers, to kiss and suck and lick, all at once. The combination of simultaneous tenderness and roughness was for me the most powerful aphrodisiac. I closed my eyes to savour the sensations. My body was on fire. Suddenly, he jerked my head to one side and pushed his rigid cock into my mouth, pushing and pumping forcefully, almost choking me. My jaw ached as he fucked my mouth, grunting and muttering, 'Filthy bitch,' but the position of my head and neck made it impossible for me to move. Finally, after one more violent thrust, he spilled his load down my throat. Seeing I could hardly breathe, he let go of my hair and pulled out abruptly. There was too much to swallow, and as I collapsed onto the rug, sticky juices dribbling down my chin and neck, he dipped his finger in and licked it. 'Not as tasty as you,' he concluded, adding, 'Honestly, what some people will do to make a sale.'

I sighed. 'I need a drink.'

'Thought you just had one.'

'Silver tongue, aren't you?' I laughed, struggling to stand on my wobbly legs.

As we sipped Coca Cola on the rug, still hot and sweaty, he said, 'You looked really sexy on that pole.'

'Thanks.'

'In fact, I would love it if you could give me a repeat performance.'

'Now?'

'Now. And this time I'll be ready for you.' He produced a shiny condom wrapper from the pocket of his jeans.

'I hope there's plenty more where that came from,' I grinned.

He unzipped his jeans to reveal deliciously snug-fitting black boxers. 'There certainly is.' He rolled over on to his stomach so I could see the full glory of his wonderful tattoos, which covered his shoulders, back and snaked right down to the groove at the top of his gorgeous tight bum. I was in heaven.

'Say something,' I murmured dreamily.

'Like what?'

'Anything.'

'You're a horny slut, Katy Bliss,' he purred.

'And you're a sexy Welsh dragon, Rhiddian Davies,' I whispered, before turning him over and clamping my mouth over his already stirring cock.

I wanted to eat him – all of him. I wanted that big hard cock inside me. I sucked and massaged with my tongue, teasing the tip, restraining myself from sinking my teeth in, instead letting them graze down the thick shaft.

'Mmmmm,' we both groaned in unison. When my mouth was filled to capacity, he withdrew swiftly, and I positioned myself on all fours, pushing my pert arse provocatively at him. He pushed my crumpled, damp skirt up around my hips and within seconds, I could feel his rock-solid cock entering me doggy style, thrusting energetically and purposefully, alternating slow, measured thrusts with rapid, hard jerks. I moved my hips rhythmically in response, as if his cock was my pole and I was circling it and gripping it with my muscles.

'Now this is what I call pole dancing,' I gasped.

We pole danced like this for the next hour or so, exhausting each other. After our third dance, when we were sprawled across the sofa, hot and sticky, I glanced at my watch. 'I'm afraid I have someone else viewing the flat,' I said. 'In ten minutes, to be precise.'

'Male or female?' he asked mischievously.

'Male.'

'Boy, is he in for a surprise,' he teased.

'What a nerve. As if I would –'

'– seduce all your prospective buyers? Dirty bitch. And as if you hadn't guessed, I love dirty bitches. The dirtier the better.'

I stood up, smoothing my skirt down, while he pulled his jeans back on. The flat reeked of sex. I would have to spray the air freshener around, and pretty quickly.

But before he put his vest back on, I had a question. There were two tattooed symbols, just above his lovely right butt cheek, that he hadn't explained.

'What do these tattoos mean?' I asked, adjusting my bra straps.

He gave me a cheeky grin and in his sexy Welsh lilt whispered, 'This one means Make Love.

And this one is Bliss.'

Not in my Wildest Dreams
by Cyanne

Eight hands glided over my arms and legs in perfect rhythm, massaging out every tension, not that I had much to be tense about these days. The angelic sitar player played and played and the four therapists worked in time with the music, a fifth drizzling an exquisite frangipani oil over my naked body. I had been prepared, like a sacred offering, for the final treat, and they were in no hurry, but I was alive and tingling at the thought of what was to come. My body hair had all been painlessly waxed off, my hair conditioned with the finest products nature had to offer, my make-up lightly applied, so I was looking and feeling my best for the amazing massage that the other women had told me about so excitedly.

I opened my eyes and made eye contact with one of the masseurs, a well-built man of just nineteen or twenty, and silently pleaded with him to move things along to the next level. Though tall and muscular he averted his eyes from my gaze with a reverence bordering on embarrassment. My pussy ached from the teasing touch of four men, all working away expertly on my hands and feet, arms and legs, but so far avoiding touching my breasts, which were conspicuously naked and glistening with oil, or my throbbing pussy, which was just covered by a tiny piece of white muslin.

I craved a finger inside me, and opened my legs slightly, hoping to tempt one of them in, but they just gently pressed them together, moving effortlessly as part of the massage. I sighed deeply. I couldn't separate whose hands were whose as they moved all over my body, avoiding my pleading nipples by mere millimetres.

How did I even get here? The letter landed on my doormat, thick cream paper with embossed gold lettering, inviting me to join Rich Bitch, an invite-only, super-exclusive club for women. Sounded like another scam to me. Since winning nine million on the lottery I'd had no end of begging letters, scams, invitations to invest, to join clubs and schemes, but this one intrigued me. There was no fee to join: it was strictly free to those who could afford it. There was no website or email address; in fact when I called the number the first thing Marilyn explained to me was that all communication should be on paper or in person.

Anything electronic was too easy to intercept. It was starting to sound like a something out of James Bond, but my interest was sufficiently piqued. When I arrived at the huge house in deepest Dorset I was impressed by the cars outside. This was not your average Audi TT crowd; the club car park boasted a vintage Mercedes Gullwing, an Aston Martin Vanquish and a huge Maybach.

Inside it quickly became apparent that the ladies of Rich Bitch were about one thing: sex. Impeccably stunning female dancers swung from golden trapezes, their tricks revealing no panties under their lavish costumes, while men for every taste and predilection walked the floor offering massages and oral sex to the designer-clad assembled women as they sipped Dom Perignon. Small curtained rooms to the sides offered some degree of privacy to the women as they got their pussies licked by a man (or men!) of their choice, reclining on velvet chaise-longues with their dresses pulled up to their waists.

I stood wide-eyed at the spectacle but was quickly found by Marilyn who came over to introduce herself. She motioned to an ornate fountain and said that if I wanted to stay I was to throw my panties in there so that I could enjoy any of the men and women on offer whenever I wanted. It was all too bizarre but I was so turned on by the goings-on that I slipped out of my thong and threw it to join the other scraps of Agent Provocateur and La Perla's finest floating in the foam, to the applause of the other women.

My short summer dress flipped at my thighs as Marilyn showed me around the house, and even though the dancers' legs were akimbo in an aerial display of pussy, I was still self-conscious as I followed her up a long staircase.

She showed me private rooms, each with its own theme. A fetish room with a love swing and bondage cross, a Lomi Lomi therapy room with a massage couch scattered with flowers, a red light room with a mirrored ceiling and a dance pole, a room with a vast Jacuzzi and sauna, a room covered in plastic sheeting with shelves and shelves of bottles of oil and different coloured lube … Never in my wildest dreams had I imagined such a place existed.

That first night, after surrendering my panties and my car keys, I got into the swing of things. A man in his thirties, dressed in a tux but with the body of an MMA fighter, walked over and asked if there was any way he could service me. I faltered a little at first, not really accustomed to this kind of forthrightness, and asked him for a foot massage. He led me into one of the small curtained rooms and delicately removed my shoes, caressing my feet one by one, applying just the right pressure to the balls of my feet. He began to kiss my feet, and looked up at me.

'Would Madame like anything else?' he asked.

I opened my legs a fraction, aware of how wanton my pussy must look with a dress but no panties. He kissed his way up my legs, his shaved head gently grazing my thighs, and softly parted my lips with his tongue, and I was in heaven. He licked so expertly, I came in minutes, thrashing against his face.

Hands starting to gently touch my breasts brought me out of my reverie and back into the massage room. Many months and countless steamy encounters had passed since my first tentative foray into the world of Rich Bitch. Two masseurs were now stroking my breasts while the other two continued to work on my feet. The sensations in my nipples made their way down to my pussy, the only part of my body they hadn't yet lavished with attention. The light fingers on my oiled nipples had me lightheaded when one of them whispered that I should turn over. I groaned with pleasurable frustration and did as they asked.

Without breaking their stroke, the masseurs' hands roamed the backs of my legs and grasped my bum. Warm oil was trickling down my spine and coming to rest between my legs, mingling with my juices as my pussy readied itself for the first touch.

The hands were dizzying, dipping just slightly further inside my thighs with every stroke, and slowing down to an excruciatingly slow pace. Finally, I felt a finger graze my hairless pussy lips and I moaned into the pillows. Another one separated them just a touch and lightly touched the tip of my clit, then another pressed just inside me. I widened my legs and lifted slightly up onto my knees, and their hands were all over my pussy, coming at me from above and below. More oil drizzled and a finger touched my arsehole, making me jump, before relaxing on to it as it slid inside. Another one went into my pussy while a third lightly but relentlessly stroked my clit. I came hard, face pressed into the pillows, and their hands supporting me as I collapsed back down. Light strokes continued over my legs and back until I signalled that was enough.

The men left and my maid, a Thai girl wearing just a little skirt and jewellery, came into the room and showered me in the wet room, rubbing right up against me as she scrubbed the oil off my skin, and making sure I got a good look at her pussy when she bent over to pick up handfuls of salt scrub.

I dressed in a simple black dress, no panties of course, and my maid repaired my hair and make-up. When I left the Lomi Lomi room, men came up to me constantly, offering their services, and I said 'maybe later' to all of them. I wanted to explore a little.

In the main hall members in cocktail dresses were dancing with the attending men while sushi was served on a naked girl lying motionless on a table in the centre of the room, and a waitress served Champagne wearing just a tiny white apron and black high heels. A couple of exceptionally submissive men were sitting on the floor with their tongues out, offering oral sex to anyone who cared to come over and shove their pussy in their faces, which most of the women – even the Champagne waitress! – took advantage of at some point in the evening.

I decided to take a peek in the dark room, somewhere I hadn't yet explored, but where entrance meant consent. I knocked on the door as the sign requested and a voice on the other side asked whether I consented to join in and be taken in whatever way the other inhabitants of the room saw fit. I'd enjoyed having hundreds of men and the occasional woman at my beck and call for the last few months, licking, massaging, fingering me any way I wanted, doing anything I asked, but I was ready to relinquish a bit of control.

'I do,' I said.

The door swung open and it was dark inside, with just a tiny black light in one corner lighting up an eerie purple area where three or four people rolled all over each other on a huge couch. The door was hardly shut when the first hands grabbed at me, handling my breasts roughly, something I hadn't felt in ages after the respectful touches of the masseurs and the submissive men downstairs. My body responded to the display of masculine power and I leaned backwards into a pair of strong arms which folded across me, holding my breasts tight and rubbing my nipples. Another pair of hands pulled my skirt up roughly and grabbed my pussy as though sizing me up. They were tearing at my dress, pulling it in all directions until it was ripped and just hanging around my waist. A face buried into my pussy, sucking so much more roughly than I was used to and I squirmed, trying to lessen the intensity, but the man behind me held me tight, biting on my neck, pulling my head back by my hair and kissing me roughly.

My feet were lifted off the floor and I was suspended between the two men, dizzy with sensation and disorientation from the darkness. They pulled me around harshly, turning me over and opening my legs wide.

A cold dollop of lube made me gasp and the men yanked me into a kneel on the floor. One man pushed me from behind, making my legs sprawl wide on the floor, and got hold of handfuls of flesh on my hips, guiding me down onto his cock. It was dark and I wriggled to angle it so it went in my pussy, but he had other ideas and pushed straight into my arse. I screamed with shock and pleasure and he pulsed inside me, biting my shoulders. A mouth was suddenly on mine, hands on my tits, and the other man was in front of me. The darkness was warm but claustrophobic and I felt smothered between these two strong bodies and gasped for breath over his shoulder. He pushed me back and forced his body up against mine, pushing his cock inside my pussy. I'd never felt anything like it, jammed between two men, two cocks inside me, the three of us moving together, our sweat mingling. Their thrusts and bites tipped me over the edge and I came over and over again.

I was disengaging myself from the sweaty tangle when a weird electronic noise invaded my thoughts. I opened my eyes into a dark room, but a different one. The men were gone, at least I think they were, and I was covered with a duvet. I was confused for a moment, and then reality seeped in. My mobile phone flashed and buzzed on the table, trying to dance its way off the library book it was

23

resting against as it did its best to wake me from my lusty slumber. The boiler above my bedroom wheezed as my housemate took a shower and I could hear the neighbours shouting at each other as they tried to jumpstart their VW Polo again. Ah well, I thought it was all a bit too good to be true, but maybe I could pick up where I left off tonight....

Confession
by Kristina Wright

Please excuse my bluntness, but I need to confess
something: I hooked up with my boyfriend's father
last Friday. *My boyfriend's father*.

There. I admitted it.

I'm blushing, just thinking about it. What the
hell is wrong with me? I'm horny, that's what it is.
I've been celibate for two months because my
boyfriend Richard has been working for his
company's office in Amsterdam while I'm in
Seattle. It's a six-month assignment and I thought I
could handle it, but I'm lonely. And horny. It's not
much of an excuse, but there it is. I let myself do
something I would never, ever do under normal
circumstances. The worst part is, I think I would
do it again. I know I would, actually. If he would
let me.

I don't know why I feel like I need to defend
myself. I didn't initiate what happened, so I could
say it wasn't my fault. Except, I feel bad because I

25

don't feel bad. I enjoyed it, I had fun and, heaven help me, I'd do it again. Does that make me a slut? Does it make me a slut that I didn't actually have sex with him, I just gave him a blowjob? Does it make me a slut that I have never felt so submissive in my life as when he told me to suck him? Does it make me a slut that I enjoyed giving him a blowjob and was practically glowing when he told me I was a good girl and it was the best blowjob he'd ever gotten in his life?

Yeah, that's what I thought.

So be it, I'm a slut. I'm also a photographer, a pretty damn good one, which is how it all got started in the first place. Richard's dad called me a week ago about doing some portraits of him and his wife for their thirtieth wedding anniversary. They didn't have professional portraits done when they got married, so he wanted to surprise her with a studio session. I don't remember everything that was said, but somehow we ended the conversation with him planning to come over and look at my portrait portfolio on Friday afternoon. The thought of him being in my apartment made me a little nervous, but it had nothing to do with sex. He has, I don't know how else to say it, a dominant personality. He talks, people listen. Me included. There's something about the way he looks at me when he talks... I don't know. I never saw myself as the submissive type, but I find myself wanting to please him in a way I've never wanted to please Richard.

I never really considered it before, but Richard's dad (his name is George, but for some reason I can't think of him as anything but 'Richard's dad') is very attractive and in shape for a guy in his fifties, with this sexy streak of white in his wavy black hair. Richard looks a lot like his dad, actually, so I guess it shouldn't surprise me that I'd be attracted to the guy.

He came over right on time for our appointment and I offered him a glass of wine. I always have a couple of glasses of wine when I get home from work, sometimes a little more on the weekend. In any case, by the time he'd finished looking at my portraits and had moved on to my more artsy stuff, we'd killed nearly two bottles of wine. Maybe that's why I didn't even hesitate when he picked up my portfolio of nudes, most of them self-portraits.

I didn't blush when he flipped to an eight-by-ten photo of me stretched naked across a hardwood floor. He studied it intensely and then looked at me. I don't know what I expected, a compliment or a thoughtful critique of the lighting, but not, 'This is my kitchen floor.'

Fuck. I'd forgotten I'd borrowed Richard's

parents' house one day last summer while they were in the Virgin Islands. I had wanted to use the fabulous natural light at their house for some self-portraits and Richard had been a more than helpful assistant. It suddenly all came back to me: setting up my equipment, stripping down, setting the timer as I changed positions while Richard watched from the kitchen table. When the light faded, we ended up rolling around on that hardwood floor, fucking like sex-starved teenagers. I couldn't tell his father all of that, of course, so I just nodded.

'Richard told me you were a very … mmm … sexual woman.'

I didn't know how I felt about Richard discussing our sex life with his *father*, but the way he looked at me nearly melted my panties. I squirmed in my chair, unable to meet his gaze. Of course, with my eyes down I couldn't help but notice the huge erection he had. I gasped involuntarily, feeling like I had done something wrong even though he was the one sitting there with the enormous boner.

'It's your fault,' he said gruffly, putting aside my portfolio. 'Don't you think you should do something about it?'

I looked at him. I knew I should tell him to fuck off, but I didn't. I couldn't. Something about his voice and the way he was looking at me made it impossible to do anything but nod.

The next thing I knew, his pants were undone and I was discovering that the phrase 'like father like son' applies to dicks as well as personalities. Richard's dad has the nicest, thickest cock I've seen in a long, long time. It might even be a little bigger than Richard's, though I find it hard to contemplate the two of them without wanting to fuck them both at the same time. I know that will never, ever happen, but a girl can dream, right?

He stroked his cock while I watched, sitting there at my kitchen table like it was the most normal thing in the world. I kept thinking about Richard and how this was his father and that I should be screaming at him to leave and calling my sweet, loving boyfriend … but I didn't say any of that. Without being told, I slipped to my knees in front of him.

His hand stilled on his cock, a pearly bead of pre-cum poised on the broad tip. Time seemed to stop while he stared into my eyes. I wanted to lean over and suck him, get it over with, but I was waiting for something. Permission, I guess. Or maybe an order.

'Do you want to suck me?' He stared at my mouth. 'Tell me.'

I nodded again. I seemed unable to speak. My mouth was dry and I licked my lips. It wasn't meant to be sexual, but he stroked his cock almost involuntarily.

'Then suck me, show me what you want.'

I whimpered low in my throat as I scooted between his knees. With a deep, steadying breath, I lowered my head and took him between my lips. I could only take the head in my mouth because he still held his cock, his fingers circling it below the broad tip, pointing it at my open mouth. His pre-cum tasted sweet and dissolved on my tongue before I'd had enough. I tried to slide my lips down, take more of him in my mouth, but his fingers restricted me. I whimpered again.

'Just the head,' he said. 'That's all you get. Suck the head.'

I swirled my tongue around the tip before sucking him like he wanted. Just the head, my lips butting up against his fingers, trying to force him to move back and give me more. He wouldn't move.

'You want it?' he asked, his voice deep. Sounding so much like Richard's voice, but rougher. 'You want more of that cock?'

I moaned around the head of his dick in my mouth. I sucked harder, licking the tip frantically. I did everything to let him know what I wanted so I wouldn't have to actually tell him.

He wrapped my ponytail around his hand and

pulled my head back. His cock made an audible pop as it slid out of my mouth. 'Tell me,' he demanded.

My lips were wet with saliva and pre-cum. I licked them, tasting him. So sweet. So nasty. I felt as if I was looking at this scene from outside my own body and I was both horrified and aroused.

'Let me suck you.' I sounded breathless and needy.

'Why?' he asked, with a tug of my hair.

I gasped. 'I need to. Please.'

'Need to do what?'

This was driving me crazy, which is exactly what he intended. He wanted me so hot and needy that I would beg, beg to please him, beg to satisfy him, beg to suck him. I was soaked through my jeans and panties, as hot and needy as I'd ever been in my life, and all I could think about was the taste and feel of him in my mouth. I looked up into his eyes and I begged.

'I need to suck your dick. Please let me suck it.'

I was rewarded with a groan and his hand tugging me toward his crotch. 'Suck it,' he said. 'Suck it good, sweetheart.'

I fell on his cock like a starving woman, my hands braced on his muscular thighs. I swirled my tongue around the head before taking more of him in my mouth. His breathing quickened and he fisted his hands in my hair, pulling it up hard from the nape of neck in just the way I liked. He let me control the depth, but he controlled the pace, moving me up and down on his cock, fucking my mouth.

'Take it deeper,' he whispered. 'I know you want it. Do it.'

He was right, I wanted it. I obeyed, taking as much of him into my mouth as I could, until I was almost deep-throating him. I pulled back only when I started to gag a little, which seemed to turn him on even more.

'Good girl, take it all. Do it.'

His praise aroused me as much as his thick cock between my lips. Slowly, so slowly, I could feel every ridge and vein as I took him down my throat. I knew he was watching me, watching me suck him like the slut I had become. I kept hearing a little voice in my head saying this was Richard's father and telling me what a horrible person I was for betraying my boyfriend like this. Instead of deterring me, it only made me suck him faster, take him deeper. At that moment in time, the only thing I wanted was for him to come down my throat and tell me how good I was for taking it all.

I felt his cock pulse in my throat and I resisted the urge to pull away. He was gripping my head so tightly, I couldn't have moved if I tried. Then he was coming, pushing his cock so far down my throat that I gagged, but I didn't pull away. I clung to his thighs as his cock twitched and pulsed. I swallowed to keep from choking, but there was nothing to taste because he was in the back of my throat.

'That's it, good girl, swallow it all,' he commanded.

I took everything he gave me, so close to orgasm that when I jerked open my jeans and touched my clit, I exploded even while he was still fucking my mouth. I gasped and moaned around his cock, dribbling spit and cum as I came and came and came. Finally, I pulled back, swiping at my mouth with the back of my hand. He was breathing hard, his hands still twisted in my hair.

We looked at each other and it was as if there was a strange connection between us now. We both spoke at once.

'Don't tell my wife.'

'Don't tell Richard.'

We laughed. What else could we do? It was so fucking surreal.

He cupped my chin in his hands. 'You're a very bad girl, aren't you?'

Even though it was over, I was still under his spell. I nodded, hesitantly. I could feel tears

33

pricking behind my eyelids.

He brushed my bangs out of my eyes and smiled. 'You're very, very good at being bad. I like that.'

I couldn't help myself. I smiled. 'Thank you.'

I should be over it. I should just let it go and write the whole thing off as a moment of temporary insanity. I definitely shouldn't ever do it again. But I'm sitting here, soaking wet from the memory of how Richard's father made me feel with just his words, and I want more. I want to pick up the phone and call him. I want to ask him to stop by my house when he gets off work. I want to do anything he wants me to do.

I want to be a very good bad girl for him.

The Window Cleaner's Boy
by Carmel Lockyer

Once a month, Sandown Associates gets its windows cleaned. Once a month, the women in my department get their fantasies fulfilled. Me too. I'm not any different to, or any better than, anybody else.

It's the window cleaner's boy, of course. And he *is* gorgeous. As soon as their cradle appears outside the seventh floor window, the sound begins – a whole room of women licking their lips and touching their hair and undoing another button on their blouse so their cleavage shows. All done, almost unconsciously, while their eyes are glued to the window cleaner's boy.

And he is worth watching. He has narrow hips that widen into rippling abs and continue on up to wide shoulders and a strong neck. On his right arm he has a dragon tattoo in emerald green. On his left cheekbone he has a small black mole, like a beauty spot. He has black hair. He smiles and stares into our eyes, one by one, as his boss's chamois soaps the window, softening us up, driving us to think dirty thoughts while he makes our windows clean. Then the window cleaner's boy lifts his squeegee and begins to cut through the bubbles and water. His face appears with each sweep, intent, his lower lip caught by his straight white teeth in a moment of unself-conscious concentration. His fingers are long, his knuckles often laced with white as the bubbles fly from the window and back against him. Dark spots of flung water appear on his T-shirt and his old, soft, pale denims. The water makes the fabric cling to his body, wrapping itself around him like a lover's caress, the jeans sticking to his thighs and groin. Anybody getting hold of him would have to peel those jeans from his skin. Any woman lucky enough to be able to undress him, that is.

I don't think I can stand it any more – I can't bear the concentrated attention of a dozen women on one man. I'm driven mad by his studied refusal to pick one of us out, to flirt, to even hint at which he prefers: blonde, brunette, slim, buxom, bold, shy? He leaves us all in the same position – unsure, unsatisfied, hankering.

I get up. Nobody notices. Nearly a dozen pairs of eyes are pinned to the window cleaner's boy. In a few minutes they will have a break from their fixation as the cradle disappears again, while the two men change the water in their buckets. Their object of lust will then return to rinse the windows and polish them. His arms will make wide arcs on the glass: glass so shiny that it hardly seems to be there, so insubstantial that you feel you could reach out and slide your fingers through it to touch the hollow of his neck, so that he stops moving and turns to gaze at you with his grey eyes, while you let your fingers trail down his body to the water-spattered jeans.

I walk fast. There isn't that much time. Sod the lift, I take the stairs, two at a time. On the first, fourth and eighth floors there are toilets for men. On the third, fifth and ninth floors there are toilets for women, where we spend our time inspecting our faces, watching our summer tans fade, admiring each other's new winter boots as we apply lippy and swap stories. But I am heading for the eighth floor. That's where the cleaners empty the buckets of soapy water and refill them with water that contains a negatively ionised liquid that supposedly stops our office windows collecting dirt. It is this magic fluid that the window cleaner's boy polishes across our view, as though he's making our desires gleam.

He comes out of the toilets as I reach the corridor and gives me a faintly startled, faintly smug smile. It's the third time he's seen me in the flesh, not through a window. Of course he thinks I've skittered down here in my business heels just to get a closer look at him, so I pause and put my hand to my chest, as though surprised, and his eyes drop to my breasts in their black silk shirt and then rise again, with more of a smile this time. Of course he thinks my tightly crinkled nipples and my lust-darkened eyes are due to him. Of course he does. He's meant to.

The window cleaner's boy moves gracefully past me to the open window, where he climbs out and operates the cradle mechanism, descending from my view. Eleven women await him, licking their lips, twisting their hair, wriggling in their computer chairs. It's become some kind of feeding frenzy, the way they lust after him. I don't think some of them even fancied him at first, just went along with the flow, but now, one woman getting hot is enough to set the others off, so he's the focus of a mass outbreak of feminine libido. I started it. I did it deliberately. So that I could do this.

I walk through the door of the men's toilet. The window cleaner is there, whistling tunelessly through his teeth as he rinses out the buckets. He sees me in the mirror. He smiles.

The window cleaner is not like his boy. He has short grey hair and blue eyes. He is trim and stocky, like a lot of men who work outdoors, and he has a permanently tanned face with laugh lines and crow's feet, caused by squinting into the sun. He wears a grey, long-sleeved sweatshirt and jeans, and the overall impression is one of greyness, mediocrity, a background blur on which the bright image of his boy shines even brighter. That suits me fine. Around his waist the window cleaner has a pocketed apron which contains his chamois and gloves, and a spatula for scraping stains from the glass. The apron fastens with Velcro, and it is the ripping sound of it being undone that marks the start.

'Seven minutes,' says the window cleaner, dropping his apron to the floor.

I nod and unzip my business skirt, already walking backwards into the cubicle behind me. We have seven minutes before the window cleaner's boy finishes polishing the seventh floor windows.

Under the skirt I am wearing only stockings and suspenders, and the window cleaner's soft hands find the flesh of my buttocks, pulling me to him as he kisses me, kicking the door closed behind us. I thought his hands would be rough, like any other workman's, but they are in water all day which makes them softer than mine, softer than any other man's. Soft, but strong. He lifts me a few inches in the air and holds me there while he nuzzles my neck.

Seven minutes isn't long, but we've got this down to an art. His kisses make me wetter than ever and I reach down and unzip his jeans, ready to take him inside me, as soon as I've slipped the condom from my jacket pocket over his cock. He unbuttons my top as I slide the rubber onto him, and lets his kidskin fingers play with my breasts until I shiver with pleasure.

I turn, lowering the toilet seat and bracing my arms on the cistern top. He pauses, and I know he is admiring the picture, my splayed legs in high-heeled shoes, the stockings and suspenders, the smart office shirt now hanging loose on either side of my naked breasts. I know he is working himself gently, running his fingers over the condom, as he takes in the contrasts between efficiency and lust, executive power and complete submission. I wriggle my hips, not wanting to lose any more time, and he chuckles as he presses the head of his shaft against me.

'You're impatient,' he murmurs in my ear as he leans forward and cups my breasts with his hands, slipping himself inside me so assuredly that it's almost as if he's always been there.

'I don't like to waste time,' is all I manage to say before I feel my muscles starting to lock around him and my hips beginning to work, milking him. I put one knee up on the toilet seat and let the fingers of my right hand begin to stray, stroking my belly, teasing out my pubes, heading inevitably for the tiny pleasure centre that will bring me off.

The window cleaner sweeps my hair to one side and bends closer, nibbling my earlobe, which always drives me insane with pleasure. I hear myself beginning to moan and beg, the sounds echoing wildly around the tiled spaces of the toilet. If any man comes in here now, we're done for, but that danger adds to the frenzy. I let go of my clit and reach further back between my legs, scraping my fingernails over his balls. He groans, but he's still in control enough for his fingers to replace mine, rubbing my bud until it flowers into orgasm.

I come once, fast, and then again, slowly, easing myself up and down the length of his cock while he stands there, his hands on my hips, watching me do all the work. I can imagine his view, his shaft in the black condom appearing and disappearing, my arse sliding to and fro. Imagining how much he likes this picture helps me to come again, although my legs are starting to cramp from the effort of sex in this tiny space, in this hurried fashion. As soon as he feels my muscles starting to clench and release, he begins to thrust, moving faster, hissing as he urges my orgasm on, so that I come just before he does.

I feel my knees beginning to soften, my back starting to droop under the strain, and then I hear a sound. It's the main door opening. I twist my head to look up at the window cleaner, who winks at me, unhurried, unworried.

He pulls out slowly, with his hand over my mouth to stop me gasping. He helps me straighten up. I try to button my shirt, but my hands are shaking and he has to help me, grinning at my incompetence.

Then he crouches, holding open the skirt I dropped on the floor, and I step into it, trying to be silent. He pulls it up, zipping it, helping me tuck in the shirt, and only then does he fasten his own flies, lifting the toilet seat to drop the used condom. He leans over, kissing me softly, open mouthed, as he presses down the toilet flush, closes the lid, and then unlocks the door and steps out, whistling.

'All done, lad?' I hear him say as he runs water in one of the sinks. I slide down to a sitting position on the toilet seat, feeling the cold nylon of my skirt's lining pressing against the hot wetness of my bare sex.

'Sure,' says the window cleaner's boy. 'No problem.'

'Right. Then we're done here for the month.'

The window cleaner pulls on the rotary towel and whistles again as he dries his hands.

I sit for a while longer, and then head back to my office. The girls are all keen to tell me what I've missed, and I nod and smile, but I didn't miss anything. They are the ones who miss out every month, not me.

Confidante
by Beverly Langland

Danielle isn't as bad as everyone makes out. I'm not as good. Appearances, as they say, can be deceptive. To look at me you'd think butter wouldn't melt in my mouth. Yet, I allow men to do despicable things to me. I often find myself in degrading situations. Unbelievably, I actually thrive on the humiliation. Yes, I'm every woman's nightmare – the submissive slut who perpetuates the myth of women as sexual objects. Yet, I am not a person confused by my sexuality or my position in society. I am well educated, culturally refined, and feel at ease among the higher echelons with whom Danielle and I spend most of our time socialising. I have the confidence to understand that within reason I can be whatever I like. I'm also discreet. I like to think that is why Danielle chose me as a companion. It isn't. It's because I allow him to ill-treat me. You can call me whatever names you like. I already know exactly what I am. Just don't ask me to explain why.

I met Danielle at an Embassy ball. He was with a young redheaded girl so timid she clung to his arm as if fearful of falling off her ridiculously high heels. I realised exactly what she was as soon as I drew close enough to look into her eyes. There was an instant spark of recognition between us and she gripped Danielle's arm tighter. She could see beneath my polished exterior and considered me a threat. I soon understood why. Danielle, an Italian living in London, explained that he was looking for a new 'confidante'. The coded message wasn't particularly subtle and later he slipped his business card into my hand. Danielle has a way with words and as soon as we spoke more privately on the telephone and I heard his sexy accent, he had me hooked.

As always, when I first meet someone new I introduce him to my friends. You can never be too careful. I like nasty men, but I don't want to end up in a black bin liner somewhere. My friends gave Danielle the thumbs-up though understandably they found him disagreeable and somewhat presumptuous in the way he openly fondled me. I actually liked his candid display of confidence, so we agreed on a second meeting. Again somewhere in public. He asked about my

fantasies, so I told all. Not as you tell a loved one –
only revealing what you think they want to hear. I
told the truth. Of past men, my brief flirtation with
women, my love of exposure, I even revealed
details of my young masochistic dabbling. Most of
all we talked of my submissive desires. The last
was of course obvious to us both. We had been
playing the game of cat and mouse since our first
meeting, but this had been the first time I had
admitted my feelings outright. It felt good to say
the words out loud. I felt free. Maybe this sounds
strange to those who do not understand, but I was
free to be a slave. His slave. This would be my
choice. However, we never talked in such terms.
Danielle doesn't like the idea of having a slave. He
prefers to call me his confidante. It makes no
difference to me what he calls me as long as I am
his. People have called me far worse in the past. I
have been someone else's 'pet', another's 'bitch'.
The last relationship didn't work out for my *master*
broke the bond of trust. Once broken it can never
be regained and everything crumbles. Therefore,
I'm alone and for someone like me that is truly
unbearable.

We arranged a third meeting, a sort of
interview to test our compatibility. Danielle told
me exactly what I should wear. A short black
leather skirt with cotton blouse, the material to be

47

ivory – not cream or white – with four small buttons. Lemon underwear, silk, but not overly decorative. Black shoes with one strap and three-inch spiked heels. So here I am. I have spent the past week shopping to make certain I look just right. Now, standing in front of him in the unfamiliar surroundings of his apartment while he checks my attire, I feel irrationally nervous. He notices. 'Why, Hannah, you're trembling ...'

Danielle continues where we left off at the pub, asking more questions, listening carefully, taking note of my answers. I tell him my darkest desires, tell him I want to realise those fantasies. If anyone can make them happen, I feel certain it will be Danielle. It isn't just a case of logistics or opportunity; I need someone forceful enough to *make* me do the depraved things running through my head. That is an integral part of the fantasy for me. Just as I hope it will arouse Danielle to force me to do them. I sense he wants to corrupt me and I am ripe for corruption.

'Promising. Would you like to belong to me, Hannah?' He makes it sound as if I am his little puppy. In truth I am. To him I am little more than his pet to use and play with as he pleases. A love-doll. Barbie, he noted on our first meeting, because of my oversized breasts and petite frame. So Barbie I become. I'll let him dress and play with

48

me. When I no longer please him, he will discard me like last year's Christmas present in favour of someone new. It is the way of my world. I feel a pang of regret for young Sarah, the girl I hope to usurp. She so desperately wants to please, but as far as Danielle is concerned, Sarah is old hat. I am the vogue. However, I am in no doubt that one day I too will suffer the same fate as Sarah. I can only trust that that day is a long way off.

'Yes,' I whisper. Danielle tells me to speak up so I answer again. Louder this time.

He leads me into a bedroom and opens one side of a double wardrobe. Inside is a multitude of rubber costumes. 'Will these fit?'

I inspect the costumes; decide that at a pinch I should be able to squeeze into them. They may be a little restrictive on top but I have never minded a tight fit. 'Yes.'

He waves an arm in the general direction of the clothes. 'When you are in my presence you will always be suitably attired – or naked. Now, let me see your underwear.'

I try to calm myself by taking deep breaths. My fingers visibly shake as I try to unbutton my blouse. I consciously have to steady them before they will function. I shudder slightly as the smooth material slides along my skin, dropping at my feet. Then I hook my fingers into the waistband of my skirt and shake it free until it too pools at my feet. I nimbly step out of the circle of material. Danielle makes me do a circuit of the room before telling me to remove my underwear.

I hesitate slightly as I reach behind to unclip my bra, aware of what I am about to do, the line I am about to cross. The brassiere falls to join the rest of my clothing. Danielle lets out an audible sigh as my breasts swing free, his eyes opening wide with pleasure. I am delighted I have pleased him. I feel the slightly chill air against my bare breasts; I have always loved that initial feeling of freedom. My nipples harden. I'm not sure if it is the cool air or Danielle's appreciation that caused them to stand erect. Either way, it is difficult to hide my reaction. With trepidation, I slowly slip my panties down my legs and lightly flick them to one side with my foot. I am acutely aware of my nakedness so I lightly cross my hands in front of my crotch. My body feels so alive! Every nerve end vies for attention. I can feel the gentle movement of air on my nipples, the tickle of pubic hair against the palm of my hand. Finally, I make to kick off my shoes but Danielle stops me.

I stand naked and trembling in the centre of the room while Danielle slowly circles me, examining every detail of my body with exaggerated interest. I know he intends to humiliate me with his inspection, but reason and knowing don't lessen the effect of his roaming eyes. A flush creeps on to my cheeks as he has me open my mouth to show my teeth, and then stick out my tongue for inspection. He even gives each of my bottom cheeks a tentative slap as if to measure their responsiveness. I take all this in my stride, though my heartbeat quickens as Danielle cups both my breasts, weighing them in his hands, measuring the girth of my nipples with his nimble fingers. They grow instantly with his touch. Finally, he runs his fingers into my bush. I feel warm digits on my slick folds, delving into my pussy, gently brushing my clit. 'You need a shave.' I blush beetroot deep with embarrassment. It is the bane of my life that I am hirsute. The thought of letting Danielle shave me makes me tremble. 'Or we could try plucking?'

My stomach lurches. I am appalled. He can't mean it. My heart races in a confused beat of fear and excitement. I feel the familiar tingle of anticipation. Or is it anxiety? The moistness in my pussy confuses the issue. I want to say something, to protest! In the end, I stand mouth agape, eyes wide in disbelief. Danielle smiles, pushes my jaw closed with his finger. 'Don't worry, Barbie. I'm not *that* cruel. Maybe just one or two if you're a good girl! Of course, at some point we will have to discuss your capacity for receiving pain.' He opens the other side of the wardrobe to reveal the instruments of his trade. 'Do you prefer the paddle, whip or crop?' He selects a crop from a range hanging on the door, slices the distance between us. I am not shocked. Pain is my friend. I feel confident I can surprise him should he decide to test me.

'OK, Hannah, you're doing fine. You have a safe word?' He smiles warmly and I try to smile back as best I can, moving to relax the stiffness in my shoulders. I have already begun to distinguish when Danielle is in character and when he isn't, like now. He is offering me another opportunity to back out if I don't want to go further. I can't beg off now that things are starting to get interesting. I want to go on. I *need* to go on. 'Rosebud,' I whisper. He doesn't ask why I chose that particular word and I offer no explanation. It was my grandmother's name and as a child she always made me feel safe and secure. It didn't dawn on me that in the current context it may be inappropriate.

'On my next command you will squat on your haunches with your hands behind your back. Do you understand?' I nod my head in assent. The position is a 'standard'. I don't have time to consider further. 'Barbie. Sit!' To squat naked in front of someone is harder than the simple act implies. It is humiliating, yet somehow never feels wrong, at least that's what I tell myself. I feel the familiar tingling in my midriff as I slowly sink to rest on my haunches. It is almost impossible for my legs not to open and I catch the aroma of my excitement. Danielle steps closer and lifts my chin with the end of the crop. I allow him to position me; back erect, head up, my breasts jutting out in front. It is difficult to maintain balance in the heels with my back straight so I have to part my legs further. Danielle considers me for a moment and then taps the crop between my knees, indicating that I should open wider still. My legs begin to shake, partly from their stretched position, but mainly from the reaction to my lewd display.

I would be lying if I say I have never exposed myself like this before. Yet, no matter how often, the sensation never diminishes. I rest open and exposed. My labia feel huge, bloated with the rush of blood to my genitals. I am acutely aware that the lips have separated. I can feel cool air dancing on my uncovered flesh vainly trying to dissipate the furnace burning between my legs. Danielle can see all. He denies me any modesty. I try to focus on something other than my sex, but my mind refuses to be distracted. At this moment, my pussy *is* the core of my being, the centre of my universe.

Danielle isn't slow to spot my arousal. 'Are you wet and aroused, Barbie?'

I know better than to lie. 'Yes.'

'Why? Out with the truth. I want to hear you say it.'

'I like showing you my pussy.'

'Only nice girls have pussies.'

He wants me to use depraved language. All men get excited when they force me to utter foul words. Danielle is no different. He concentrates on my pretty mouth as I say, 'I like to show off my cunt!'

'That's better. And such a pretty cunt it is too.' Danielle manoeuvres the crop between my legs, pushes the end firmly against my wetness. The coarse leather swatch scratches against my clitoris, coaxing it from the safety of its hiding place. My nubbin is hypersensitive. I can feel the minute texture of the hide. I press back against it, hoping the movement is subtle enough that Danielle won't notice. His smile indicates otherwise. He removes the source of pleasure and my mind screams in protest. How long will he expect me to wait? I watch as he lifts the tip of the crop to his nose, breathes in my scent, his nostrils flaring wildly. All sense of dignity crumbles. 'Please ...'

'Would you like to touch yourself?' I want Danielle to touch me but failing that, I will settle for the opportunity to thrust my hand between my legs, to ram fingers deep into the burning flesh. My clitoris is nagging like a bad tooth and I need to ease the throbbing. I know he won't let me off that easy. Danielle will have me work for the right to climax and I can tell from his expression that I haven't earned that privilege yet. Still, I nod eagerly, hopeful that he will let me masturbate in front of him, expecting him to thwart me further. Danielle surprises me. 'As you wish. Spread yourself.'

I am thrilled that Danielle would demand such a thing. It is degrading. Horrible! Nasty! Dirty! Disgusting! By the time my mind has sorted through the list of admonishments my hands are already at my pussy, grabbing my bloated lips and spreading myself wide. Yet, rather than mollify my frustration the gentle pull only serves to stoke the fire within. It shouldn't be stimulating; clinically holding myself wide for examination, but the debauchery of the act *is* making me excited. Danielle leaves me exposed while he rummages in the wardrobe. When he returns, he brings with him two metal objects on chains, shaped almost like giant teardrops. It isn't until he bends between my legs and I see the metal clips that I fathom their function. For a man who has already told me that he gains little pleasure from inflicting unnecessary pain, the clamps look decidedly fierce. I hope their bark is worse than their bite.

As Danielle crouches close it takes all of my resolve not to shy away. I steel myself for the inevitable, so nervous I almost pee myself. Danielle sees the dread in my eyes. He hesitates with one clamp open and hovering dangerously close to my sensitive lips. 'OK, Hannah?' Again, he is asking for my permission to continue, giving me another opportunity to stop, maybe my last before the game goes too far and I run out of options. I look into his beautiful hazel eyes. It is impossible for him to hide his own arousal. How can I disappoint him? For reasons that I can't or don't want to comprehend, I trust him completely. I force a wry smile and nod my assent. It is too late to back out now; besides, the perverse masochist within me wants to know what the clamps will feel like.

I hold my breath as he attaches the first clip, biting down on my lip as the clamp squashes onto my sensitive flesh. The clamp itself is not as fierce as I had imagined, but I can feel the cold metal against my blazing flesh. Tentatively Danielle releases his hold and I feel the skin around my pussy stretch under the full weight of the teardrop. I will not deny that it is painful and tears well to my eyes. After a moment's respite Danielle repeats the procedure with the other weight. He kneels and produces two miniature weights of similar design to the larger teardrops. I know what they are immediately. I thrust my breasts forward with a keen sense of anticipation. I know from previous experimentation that I can easily withstand the pressure of the clamps on my nipples. Danielle laughs aloud at my eagerness to have my body abused. The only surprise is the tinkle of each as he attaches them. They are tiny bells! When he has finished, I can't resist jiggling my breasts to make the bells tinkle for his amusement. After all, I am his jester. His pet. My sole purpose to entertain. I feel more relaxed with the idea now. He laughs a second time, then reaches in and kisses me tenderly. I want more, want at least to feel his tongue explore my mouth, but he stands and walks away into the lounge.

He leaves me to get used to the feel of my new jewellery. Although the clamps are uncomfortable – painful even – I cannot bring myself to think of them as punishment. I have long ago come to terms with my perverse addiction to pain. Somewhere along the way, I blurred the boundary between pain and pleasure in my sex life. I can't find adequate words to describe how I feel. None adequately describe the emotions running through me. All I can be certain about is that I am fulfilling a need that lives constantly within me. A need that I have never before had the opportunity to fully acknowledge, let alone appease. Whatever else I am feeling, I am aroused beyond all reason.

It is a bizarre sensation as I crouch, exposed, clamped and stretched while Danielle busies himself with the mundane act of mixing a gin and tonic. On his return he sits in the chair opposite me, crosses his legs, which only serves to remind me of the ache in my own. I have been in the same position for a long time and my legs are already numb. All the while he had been in the lounge I had dutifully not moved. Danielle hadn't told me that I couldn't, yet I second-guessed that was his intention. After all, he hadn't told me that I could move either. I ponder if the pain I feel is therefore technically self-inflicted. It's at times like this that I have too much time to think. If only to take my mind away from the burning heat between my legs.

'OK, Barbie, on my next commands you will get down on all fours and wait. Then when I give you the instruction you will crawl to the other side of the room, retrieve your panties in your mouth and bring them back here. Do you understand?' I nod. It is clear that he wishes to humiliate me further. 'Barbie. Down!' I lean forward to the sound of tinkling bells until I am on all fours, glad to move my legs at last. Pins and needles burst through my thighs as the blood rushes back into my legs. I can feel the hard wooden floor beneath me, pressing back against my bare knees, harsh and unfeeling. The weights attached to my pussy lips swing with me, pulling insistently on my flesh, stretching me. Surely, my labia must be touching the floor. I realise how I must look to Danielle and cringe inwardly. A naked slut about to crawl for her master. I shiver in anticipation of the next command like a parent at the start of a sack race. Knowing that I am likely to make a fool of myself.

'Barbie. Fetch!' I will myself to move my hands and knees in a crawling motion. As I shift, the weights swing around, knocking together, tugging and jerking on my pussy. It is a most curious sensation. The bells attached to my nipples tinkle in a sort of complimentary tune. As I crawl away from Danielle I am aware that from behind I will be fully exposed. I can feel the cool air ruffling the hair between my legs. The harsh cold floor beneath my knees, my hands. My bare breasts swinging as I crawl, each movement accompanied by the tinkling of the bells. My humiliation rises but I keep going until I reach my pile of clothes. Then I lower my head to take my panties between my teeth. They aren't heavily soiled but the scent of my earlier excitement permeates the soft material.

The return journey is easier to bear. Danielle's smiling eyes encouraging me as he follows my approach. I can see he is pleased! I kneel beside his chair without further instruction and wait. A smile plays across Danielle's soft lips and he leans over and ruffles my hair. 'Good girl!' He pulls me against him and kisses the top of my head in a gesture that is so full of caring – so wonderfully domestic – that I nearly weep. 'Enough for one evening I think.'

No! I want more. I need to come, for one thing. Desperately! I look up at Danielle with pleading eyes. With puppy dog eyes. He doesn't have to be psychic to recognise my need. Thankfully, he offers me the promise of further humiliation. 'Time to give you that shave. Then we'll see where that leads.' It is the carrot to keep me faithful. Danielle gathers the long strands of my hair and guides me, naked and on all fours, towards the bathroom. He uses my hair as a lead, keeping me close to heel. I can't wait to feel his touch between my legs. I am so excited now. Coiled like a spring, so close to coming I am ready to rupture. As I crawl, I start to moan in anticipation. Danielle looks down on my quivering body, an amused expression on his face. He uses the crop to stop my dallying, leaving a nasty stripe across my buttocks. Please God, any further stimuli and I am sure to explode.

In the end all it takes is the gentle tug of Danielle's guiding hand entangled in my hair.

The School Reunion
by Kitti Bernetti

Jeanie'd only been waiting for this moment for twenty years. As she walked up the road to the school, it gave her goosebumps even now. The happiest days of your life. Well, maybe to some but not to Jeanie.

It's amazing how some people change, she thought, catching a glimpse of her thirty-year-old self in the window of a shop. Take her for instance. As a ten-year-old, she hadn't shown much promise either in the way she looked or her intellect. She was one of the average kids as far as brains were concerned. As far as looks went, she was one of the ones the mothers outside the school gates would look at and think, 'shame'. Jeanie could see the sympathy in their eyes as their pretty, bouncy kids frolicked with the other chosen ones. She'd look at the floor and feel guilty for taking up space. Childhood hadn't been her finest hour.

But the gods had made up for it since. Once

she got to thirteen, her hormones kicked in producing breasts that had developed faster than the blush on a schoolboy's cheek. Firm as a tightly blown up balloon, with nipples that stood out like thimbles, they'd been obscene, even under her thick school jumper. As if to make up for the misery of her early years, nature bestowed its kindest charms on the teenage Jeanie. Lustrous thick blonde hair so long it grazed her waist, legs the length of telegraph poles and an arse so mobile men were mesmerized by it. But the older Jeanie was even better, for she had added a touch of class.

She looked good tonight and she knew it. Jeanie had chosen her outfit well, because she knew he was going to be there and, whatever happened, she had to have him. She smiled at the reflection of her arse bobbing along. What man could resist that? Not many. Her white skirt was made of that clingy jersey that kisses every curve of a well-built woman. Close observation revealed the tiny thong hugging her hips. The plain black top she wore above it pretended to be prim but, all the while, the ardent observer could peer at it and see the roundness of an overfull cleavage poking through. One button left open at the top, and two at the bottom to reveal a tanned flat stomach, should hook her prey. It was going to be one special night. She felt her breasts tingle just at the thought of it.

As she entered the crowded hall there was that unmistakable whiff of cabbagey school dinners combined with sweat and the rubber of plimsolls. She wrinkled her pert little nose with distaste. Instantly one of the male staff members approached her. He was young, good-looking. Under different circumstances, she would have sparked with approval. But not tonight.

'Hi, what was your year?' he schmoozed.

'That would be telling. Just as a lady doesn't tell her age, she doesn't tell which years she was at school. It would be too easy to work out the vital statistics.'

'Especially for me. Let me introduce myself. Lee Sheffield, I teach maths here.'

'Lucky you,' she smirked.

'Can I show you around? Or get you a drink, maybe?' His attention was flattering. It was a shame to waste him but she had bigger fish to fry. She trawled around instead looking for the object of her desire. He wasn't in this mob. 'Is the reunion taking place just in this hall or is it spread around the school?'

'Next door as well, in the science wing.' *Of course. That was where he'd be.*

'Thanks, I know where that is.' As she made to move off, he cornered her. 'I'd really like to reminisce with you about old times.' *Wow that was a crap chat-up line but, hey, these weren't normal circumstances and that tousled hair and those faded jeans straining with muscles were pretty cute.* 'Maybe I could have your phone number?'

She hesitated. Jeanie hadn't got to senior sales exec and a six figure salary without being focussed and there was no one and nothing which was going to put her off her goal for tonight. Nevertheless, part of her success also sprung from being open to suggestions. She dug in her Louis Vuitton handbag and fished out a business card. She gave it to him, winked and slinked off, feeling his eyes burn into her jiggling rump as she walked.

As she entered the science block she spotted her target instantly. She'd know that angular stooped figure and that sharp nose anywhere. Okay, so he was twenty years older but basically it was the same model, just skinnier, and with now grey instead of brown hair. Beside him, unmistakably, stood his wife. A dessicated little rodent of a woman, Jeanie almost laughed out loud. Picking him up would be like taking candy from a baby if that dried-up female was the only item of womanhood he'd had to screw for the last two decades.

She wandered into his field of vision and could see she'd instantly caught his eye. He always was a letch. All the kids knew it. The way he used to hang around outside the gym pretending he was stopping the boys peering in at the girls undressing, when all the while he was guiltier than they were. It made the hair on Jeanie's neck stand on end.

Completely ignoring his wife, who was instantly engaged in small talk by one of the other old girls, Mr Sloane sidled up to Jeanie. 'Can I help you?'

'Maybe,' Jeanie twirled a skein of hair provocatively in her fingers and gave him her most heavy-lidded look. 'Why, you're Mr Sloane, the physics teacher, aren't you?'

'Yes. I can't quite place you though. What year was it?'

Oh no. She wasn't going to make it that easy for him. Besides, he might start to remember and get frightened away. 'Mr Sloane, wow. You're still looking so good.'

'I am?' The old letch was as flattered as a parading peacock. He straightened himself and ran a finger through his thinning hair.

'Absolutely. I'm sure old pupils come up and tell you this all the time, but, guess what, I had such a crush on you.'

'That's interesting.' He wiped a little bit of spittle from the side of his mouth. She could see the old bastard falling – hook, line and sinker.

She wrinkled her nose and toyed with the top button of her blouse. Like a dog sniffing at a bitch, his eyes lit up. 'And do you know, it hasn't weakened at all with the years. In fact, if anything I'd say it was stronger.'

He swallowed and his Adam's apple bobbed up and down. 'Really. A fine young woman like you looking at an old has-been like me.' He took her arm, all over her like a rash, and directed her towards the dark passageway which ran alongside the science block. 'Would you like to see some of our new classrooms?'

'Actually,' she giggled girlishly, hoping she wasn't laying it on too thick. 'I'd really like to visit the old lecture theatre, the one right at the top of the building where you used to do most of your lessons. I remember watching you. We could sort of re-enact how it used to be. With you on the stage, and me sitting in the audience looking up at you, wide-eyed with admiration.'

'That would be fun, my dear,' he leered. 'Let's do it.'

In the lift, she deliberately stood close to him, her shoulder almost touching his arm. He looked hot, slightly sweaty, as if he couldn't believe his luck. She had to get him ready and this confined little space was ideal for the purpose. She breathed out, her full breasts like ledges. 'Is it me, or is it really warm in here?'

His eyes strayed down, and his tongue came out of his mouth and licked his lips. 'Yes, my dear, I think it is.' Mr Sloane's eyes bulged like a goldfish's as she undid a button on her blouse exposing the black lace of her bra and the very tops of her nipples.

Jeanie looked up at him and smiled. 'I often dreamed you and I might get stuck in this lift.'

It was all he needed to make the first move. Tentatively she felt his hand slide over the rounded globes of her taut arse. 'We might get stuck in it today,' his voice was thick with desire.

'Maybe,' she said moving her legs open slightly, knowing that he wouldn't let it pass his notice. His breathing was becoming grainy now, ragged with lust.

'You have the most delectable bottom I have ever seen on a young woman.'

She stuck it out and wiggled slightly. 'I'm glad you like it. Get down on your knees and you can have a sniff.'

'Yes, there's nothing I'd like more,' he grunted, kneeling down on the floor. First he fondled both cheeks in his bony hands. Clumsily he then grasped the hem of her skirt and pulled it up, revealing the eye-filling sight of Jeanie's behind in her tiny purple thong. Her arse thrust in

Mr Sloane's bristly face, and her purple suspender belt strained to hold up the flesh coloured stockings on her long shapely legs. She hoped he liked stockings because very soon, although he didn't know it, he was going to find himself tied up securely with them. He dipped his face in, roughly pulled her bum cheeks apart and sniffed, snorting like a pig.

When she felt he'd had enough to drive him insane, Jeanie pulled her skirt down and said, 'I think this is our floor. Let's go into the lecture theatre and we can have some real fun.'

He scrambled after her as she entered the double doors that led to the huge hollow room. 'This is the spotlight, isn't it?' she said, flicking on the switch and bathing the stage in light.

'You remember things well.'

'Oh yes, I remember every minute of one particular day we were in here.'

'Come with me onto the stage,' he said, 'that way I can see you better and give you what you really want.'

She winked at him, as if he was the most desirable male in the whole human race. In her large handbag, the bamboo cane she had carefully selected for the job bumped against her leg, sharp and hard. The room was silent, you could have heard a pin drop.

Jeanie placed her handbag on the table where she could grab it easily and stood behind it, just out of Mr Sloane's reach. She tossed her blonde locks and plumped her lips, thick with shiny gloss. 'I'll bet you like to play games, don't you, Mr Sloane?'

'I don't get much chance to play nowadays. My wife is a tad cold. In fact she's as icy as Antarctica.'

'Poor you,' pouted Jeanie.

He started to edge around the table and Jeanie darted away. 'I'd like to play very much,' he grinned, his beady eyes alight with desire.

'OK then. We start with you watching.' With that, she lifted her skirt so he could see her stocking tops and her muff, and placed her hand over the front, rubbing it suggestively. He was getting satisfyingly hard, she could see, as he pressed himself against the other end of the table, the slimy toad. His tented trousers displayed a tiny wet bubble. He was nearly ready.

Slowly and deliberately, Jeanie undid her suspenders and rolled the long stockings down those endless legs. Mr Sloane's mouth dropped open.

'Come here,' she breathed.

'Anything for you my dear. Anything to please you.'

She waved the stockings at him as he came nearer then said, 'Give me your wrists, you're going to be my slave.'

'Oh God,' he crooned, 'make me serve you.'

'Take your trousers off,' she ordered.

'Yes, yes.' He fumbled with the button and the zip, pulling them hastily down. 'Now your pants, and your shirt.'

His eyes goggled at her with the sheer joy of thinking she wanted to see his spidery body. As if. He was even more repulsive naked than dressed.

The arrogant bastard obviously thought he was God's gift standing there with a hard-on which jutted out like a pistol.

She smiled, backing away as he tried to touch her. 'No, no, just you wait, your reward will come in a while', and slid the still warm stocking over his wrists, tied them tightly, knotted them and led him to the hard metal bracket anchored into the wall on which the whiteboard was secured. It was perfect. He wouldn't get away from that, no matter how much she thrashed him.

Now was the time to get him really worked up. Bit by bit, she undid her buttons, watching his staring eyes drinking her in. In a second she was standing in her bra which barely held her ample breasts. He stood trembling before her. 'Take off your skirt,' he croaked.

She almost laughed out loud, who did he think was giving the orders here? Humour him, just for one minute more, she thought. In a moment, she was standing there in just her thong and high heels. His hands tied mercilessly behind his back, he strained forward to where she stood just out of reach.

'Come here,' he said, 'let me lick you.'

She picked up her handbag and walked over to him. He kneeled down, his face in line with her beautiful scented muff and stuck out his tongue.

'Not so soon,' she snarled backing away. A look of fright sparked in his eyes as he peered up at her from his kneeling position. His ramrod erection stayed taut with excitement.

'You don't remember who I am, do you?' She paced around him.

'So many girls pass through here, I couldn't remember them all could I?'

She brought her muff closer to his face and put down the bag with the cane nestling in it. The thought that she and only she knew it was there filled her with a feeling of power. Complete, total, utter power.

'I'll bet you remember the name Jeanie Powell, don't you?'

Mr Sloane frowned, wrinkles scarring his forehead. He moved uneasily on his knees, obviously in some discomfort. Good. 'Jeanie Powell. That does ring a ... you, you're Jeanie Powell?' The look of uncertainty turned to one of terror.

'It's coming back now, isn't it? That day, when you told me off for losing my homework. You said you wanted to make an example of me. Remember it?'

'I ... yes, but you were a naughty girl, you were ...'

'Shut up.' Jeanie's magnificent breasts heaved with indignation, her nipples rock hard with excitement. 'I'm not interested in hearing you justify yourself, **Mister** Sloane. I take it you remember how you told me off in front of every single person in class. How you decided to make me squirm. Remember, remember what you did?' She paced in front of him.

'Sort of.'

'Well, maybe, if you lick my shoes, you'll remember better.'

'I hardly think ...'

'Do it.'

'I'm the one used to giving orders young lady.'

'Not any more,' said Jeanie and pulled out the long hard cane from her handbag. 'Lick them.'

He stared at the cane, a look of defiance in his

eyes. 'No.'

Sharply, she brought the cane down on his skinny backside. As he shot forward with the pain and squealed, she noticed his prick get even bigger. 'Oh I see,' she said smoothly, 'you like that do you?'

Insolently he stayed silent. She pulled her arm back, to its longest extent and brought the cane crashing back down on his arse. It made a cracking sound that made her heart race. He was whimpering now.

'Lick my shoes.' He looked up at her, his face red with resentment and gingerly put out his tongue. 'That's it,' she cajoled, stroking his feeble little buttocks with the cane and imagining his arsehole tweaking in anticipation. His tongue darted out like a snake and licked. 'Faster.' The faster he licked, the more turned on she became. Gradually, knowing he was watching her, she pushed her finger inside her damp thong and started to whisk. 'I'll bet you'd like to stick your finger in here, wouldn't you? Bet you'd like to get your tongue in too.'

His eyes lit up in anticipation. 'Bet you thought that's what was going to happen when we came up here. Trouble is, Mr Sloane,' she said, rubbing away at her clit, feeling it swell and throb, 'I remember what a foul piece of work you were. I remember standing on this stage as a poor, ungainly ten-year-old and hearing you tell everyone how ugly I was. How stupid and ungainly, how pathetic I was and how I'd never amount to anything.' As Jeanie spoke, she watched his face, an expression of mingled desire and horrified anxiety. Fingering herself and watching his dick swell almost to bursting point, she thrust her muff near him, grabbing his hair in her hand and yanking him close while her finger darted in and out. As she watched with total satisfaction, his tongue darted towards her, desperate to get a taste, but she yanked him back. In one juddering movement, she came over her busy digit and, pulling it out, wiped her sticky juices all over his face.

'Now, it's your turn.'

Again, he didn't know what to think. Again, she had him totally in her power. He struggled, his wrists rubbing red and raw. She bought the cane up again, thwack and watched both his mouth and his dick twitch. Again it came up and again, sharply on his trembling buttocks. One more should do it. Again, she pulled back, her breasts bouncing with the effort and slammed the unyielding length of bamboo against his buttocks just as his prick exploded, firing hot sticky come in a jet across the stage.

His prick jerked, and shuddered and died, shrinking back till it was almost invisible.

'I've waited a long time for that,' she said, slipping her underwear, top and skirt back on. She installed the cane back neatly in her handbag and started to walk away.

Exhausted, hardly able to speak, unutterably miserable, he cried out, 'Stop. Untie me. Please, I beg you. You can't let them find me like this.'

'Why not?' She asked, strolling away. 'That was all part of the plan.'

As she walked through the double doors which led to the lift, suddenly, she heard a quiet but distinct round of applause. There, leaning against the wall in the shadows, having seen everything through the tiny glass window in the door, was Lee Sheffield, a wicked grin on his face. Jeanie flushed pink at the discovery. Would he tell? Would she get done for assault? Would he rush in and release Mr Sloane?

'That was the best bit of theatre I've seen in a long time. Jeanie, isn't it?' She looked down and saw that his crutch was swollen with a magnificent hard-on.

She smiled a wicked smile and realised that frigging herself hadn't nearly satiated her throbbing desire. 'Are you up for some fun too?'

'Sure', he said, 'but I think we'd better go to

my flat. I like to be in control when I'm around naughty little girls'. So saying, he took her bag with the cane hard inside it and led her away into the dark starless night.

Two's Company
by Georgina Brown

The bedroom door was ajar. Soft, creamy satin covered the bed. The pillows were also of satin.

The last rays of sunset picked out her head on the pillow, her hair a bluish-black against the creamy shine of satin.

On the other pillow he saw blonde hair. At first he caught his breath and felt a huge surge of anger. She had been unfaithful to him, she who had promised not to sleep with any other man unless he was present. This one had his arm around her and was vaguely familiar.

In a sudden rush of recognition, he knew it was no man lying there, but her best friend, Gloria. Both girls were asleep and doubtless naked. But to him it didn't really matter if two girls had been playing at being lovers. Una had not betrayed him.

Spellbound and clad only in his trousers now, he stared at the two beautiful women, their creamy arms thrown across each other.

Suddenly, he was smitten with the enchantment of the scene. His heart became full of love, his body full of desire.

There could be no course of action open to him except the one he had in mind. Imagine, he thought. Man's greatest desire, to be in bed between two women. The thought made him shiver. He asked himself whether they were likely to protest. He couldn't know for sure.

Test the water.

It was all he could do.

Silently, he stepped out of his trousers and what remained of his clothes.

Penis standing proud and ready, he stepped forward and got onto the bed. They murmured something as he began to edge between them, snuggling down under their entwined limbs. As he did so, he sighed loud and long and closed his eyes. If it was good to go to sleep with a woman's body up against his, it was even better when it was two women in the bed.

'What?' Una said it slowly, blearily, and opened her eyes. 'Ben! What are you doing here?'

He smiled in what he considered a disarming way. 'I wanted to see you.'

He had wanted to say 'fuck you', but decided on the softly, softly approach. Mr Romance, here I come!

His strategy obviously worked. Her body came closer, pressed against his. Her arms encircled him and her lips were on his, on his neck, on his chest.

Gloria, Una's friend, stirred behind him, her strong perfume drifting over his shoulder.

He felt the thick bush of her pubic hair against his buttocks, felt her lips on his shoulders.

'Honey,' he heard her say in a sleepy voice.

Gloria did not usually do anything for his libido, but this was an exceptional circumstance. He murmured with pleasure as the warmth of their bodies pressed more positively against his. By his presence alone, he had ignited some unseen fire in them. Their torsos undulated against him like waves against a beach.

'Keep doing that,' he murmured. 'Keep doing that for ever.'

Their hands seemed to be all over him at once. He felt he was drifting away on a tide of sheer decadence. Pleasure had become a magic carpet ride.

One female hand cupped his balls, while another pulled on his stem. Their other hands caressed his chest, his belly, and their lips landed like butterflies on his mouth, his neck and his chest.

They were pulling on him, urging his member to dance with the advance of rising semen. He was at no pains to stop them. His throat was dry, his voice trapped in his throat.

He was still lying on his side when Gloria's free hand began to caress his behind. As she did this, Una raised her leg, bent her knee and rested it over his leg. Her pussy came closer. Her sexual lips opened, and her mouth clamped swiftly over his.

Springing like a creature from cover, his prick leapt forward, its head nudging into the fleshy crack between her thighs.

It was so easy, so delicious to slide into her. With a thrust of his pelvis, half his weapon gained entry. With a second thrust, his whole length filled her body. His pubic hair rasped against hers.

All the while, Gloria's hand caressed his behind and crept into the gap between his legs to play with his balls.

The sensations from this were incredible. Gloria was manipulating his balls, not just for his benefit or her own, but also for that of Una. As Gloria's caresses became more positive, his whole body seemed to surge into Una, his penis swelling under pressure from what was happening within and without.

Every vein in his neck felt as if it were bursting. Every fibre of his being was helpless in their hands.

Just when he felt he had reached the zenith of their ministrations, Gloria's finger ran down between his cheeks and jabbed fiercely at the aperture between. He cried out, his back arching, his pelvis thudding against that of Una.

It was as if he had been speared; as if he was no more than a monkey on a stick dancing to someone else's tune.

His essence spurted out of him. Even if he had wanted to hold it back, to play for time until Una had reached her orgasm, he could not have done so.

Whatever these women wanted they would take. And whatever they wanted, he would give it to them.

Una kissed him once he was fully spent. Her fingers ran through his hair, slid down over his ear. She traced circles around its outer edge.

He looked into her eyes. Even in the semi-darkness of the room, they still sparkled. Again he felt helpless.

'Have we finished with him yet?' Una said to Gloria.

Gloria giggled behind him. Her finger was still embedded in his anus. He tried to wriggle off.

'Not so fast,' Gloria said against his ear. 'Didn't you hear what Una said? We haven't finished with you yet.'

'Greedy girls,' he said. 'What do you want now?'

Their bodies became like clothes that fitted a little too tightly.

'We're going to give you exactly what you deserve.'

They stretched his arms over his head and tied his wrists to the towering posts of the cast iron bed.

A sudden worry crossed his mind. 'Is this going to hurt?'

'Not much.' It was Gloria who answered.

He began to struggle.

Una laid her hands on his chest. Her lovely face came close to his.

'Don't worry, darling. Lie back and enjoy it, there's a good boy. If you don't, Una will smack your naughty bottom or stick things into it that it just won't like!'

Gloria got out of bed and went to the bathroom. He could hear her using the lavatory.

When she came back, she held a long, orange-coloured bottle in one hand.

'What's that?' he asked as she took out the stopper.

'Oil,' murmured Una as she flicked her fingers at his hair and kissed his brow. 'Don't look so worried. It really is only oil.'

His lips suddenly felt incredibly dry. He ran his tongue over them. They did not improve.

Gloria's fingers fastened around his limp weapon.

He groaned. 'Oh, no! Not again!'

The girls cuddled up to him.

'But darling, you've had what you came for. Now what about us?' Una exclaimed.

'That's right, darling,' added Gloria. 'You might think it's just fun going to bed with two women, but every pleasure has to be paid for. Two women are hard work – as you, my darling, are about to find out!'

To his great surprise, his stiffness returned. Una and Gloria stroked his purple-veined protrusion which was already delivering a spit of salt-laden juice from its throbbing head.

Despite his fear of not being able to perform – because fear was really what it was all about – he found himself murmuring with pleasure. Their hands were all over him, stroking his chest, his belly, nibbling at his ears, his neck and his throat.

Una's mouth covered his and suppressed the groan that accompanied Gloria's nibbling of his balls. He could feel her soft cheeks against his inner thighs, her nose against his stem.

Strong and newly virile, his penis stood up. Chest heaving, he watched as Una got astride his pelvis and lowered herself onto his phallus. Slowly but surely, the whole length was gobbled up by her body.

Beyond her he could se Gloria bent between his thighs, her bottom high in the air, her teeth still nibbling at his balls as Una rode his stem.

The urge to catch up with her and fill her with his semen was extremely powerful, but he was not given the chance.

'My turn!' he heard Gloria cry.

They swapped places.

Ben knew he was being used, but could do nothing to stop it – not that he wanted to.

The lips of Gloria's plump pussy slid down over his length.

He groaned with pleasure as Una lifted his leg and began licking from his scrotum and into his crack.

'Give me more,' he heard Gloria say.

He tried to protest. 'Girls, I can't take much more.'

They ignored him and spoke to each other.

'Is he letting you down?' Una asked Gloria.

'This stud is not doing his best,' Gloria responded.

Una sighed. 'Oh dear. Then I'll have to deal with it. Now let's see if I can find his 'g' spot again.'

Ben cried out and arched his back as Una's finger pushed into his anus. She did not ease it in, testing to see if it pained or pleasured him. She pushed it straight in up to the hilt so that his hips rose from the bed and his penis rammed home more fiercely into Gloria's accommodating vagina.

Because the response was so fierce, he could not stop the vessel that ran the length of his penis from filling up with fluid. Neither could he stop it from racing to the tip of his shaft and spilling like foaming milk into the waiting Gloria.

He groaned when Una said she wanted him to fuck her too.

'Oh come on, Ben. Isn't this what threesomes are all about? Everyone getting what they want?'

Still tied to the bed, he did as she required as best he could, though the sight of her ass and his penis disappearing between her cheeks did go some way to help.

Hours later – though it seemed longer to him – they finally untied him.

'We'll rest for now, and try again later.'

That was their plan, but it wasn't his. Once they were asleep, he eased himself out from in between them, ostensibly to go to the bathroom.

His clothes were where he'd left them. The girls were still sleeping. He was out of there.

'Two's company, three's a …' The usual phrase was that three was a crowd. In his threesome fantasy it was the girls who did the work.

On weary legs, his penis sleeping like a squashed giblet in his pants, he exited stage left.

Threesomes, he decided, were a bloody nightmare!

Looking for love? Our unique dating sites offer the perfect way to meet someone who shares your fantasies.

www.xcitedating.com

Find someone who'll turn fiction into reality and make your fantasies come true.

www.xcitespanking.com

Spanking is our most popular theme – here's the place to find out why!

www.girlfun-dating.co.uk

Lesbian dating for girls who wanna have fun!

www.ultimatecurves.com

For sexy, curvy girls and the men who love them.

Also available at £2.99

Confessions Volume 1

Some experiences just have to be confessed!

When a voyeur discovers a secret oasis of naked sunbathing girls, it's not long before the watched turn the tables on the watcher...

After learning the art of rope-play and a woman's love of vibrations in a special place, there's a guy who can get a girl to do anything, even in public ...

Who would have guessed that an uptight female teacher had such outrageous tastes? But the guy who thawed the ice-maiden learns that dirt has a special appeal ...

Hell hath no fury like a woman scorned; the trick is to learn how to love it ...

ISBN 9781907016318